AF350995

Momentary

By

Shwan Fraidoon Abdulqader

For no one.

The only chapter of the book

I went to work early in the morning. The weather was very foggy and the sky was dark and gloomy. A sign of the unsettling atmosphere in my town. As I was dressing, I heard an eerie noise coming from outside. I thought it might be a cat, its' soul leaving the physical existence of it. I wore a plain black t-shirt with skinny black jeans and a pair of white sneakers. My job doesn't require me to wear a uniform so I can dress freely. I still don't understand why some jobs mandate employees to dress in a particular way, as if they are naked objects dying to be ornamented. I walk to my workplace which usually takes a 20-minute walk. This morning the streets feel weird. No cars, no people, no noises. Everyone has disappeared. They are probably sleeping by now, dreaming about living a life full of luxury and privilege.

What a pathetic world we live in. I work in a local supermarket as a cashier. It's a part-time job.

"Good morning, Keevan"

"Good morning, Leyla. How is everything?"

She looks at me with her dark eyes, demonstrating fatigue and boredom. "as always." she mouths. It was stupid of me asking her that question. I already know everything about her since we have been working at the same place for what feels like a century. I started going behind the counter since I work as a cashier, the goal of my job is unknown. Leyla starts sweeping the sky blue-tiled floor, cleaning it as harshly as possible. In the afternoon, some old lady comes to buy some milk for her grandchildren. "Welcome" I say to her as she comes to me to pay for her stuff. She doesn't reply but I am not bothered by her attitude. I already have so much to worry about. "what day is it?" she asks. "it's Friday." I reply. She probably has Alzheimer.

After I finish at work, I walk back to my place to take a shower and then sleep. Sleeping for me is a sacred function, a fundamentally constructed path for relaxation. My body feels satisfied when I sleep. Sometimes, I sleep to dodge responsibilities. I usually sleep from 8 in the evening to 6 in the morning. Is it called sleeping at this point? "You are basically hibernating." said Leyla. She was not wrong. On Sunday morning, I go for a walk in the local park, smelling the flowers and breathing in the fresh air, free of annoying children and other creatures that contribute to the worldly irritation. There is a Persian cat in the park, moving around freely. It seems lost but at the same time liberated. At some point I feel jealous of the cat. Not having to work is a privilege that has been abandoned a long time ago. The cat seems confused, anxious and tired, but his or her freedom is unlimited. An objective for many humans to achieve.

The sky isn't fully bright as I am walking in the park. It's 5:55 in the morning. Time doesn't matter too. It is repetitive. I approach the cat to play with him. It's a male. He hisses at me. I feel threatened. Just like I always do when I encounter my boss. The cat might be a representation of my boss as well. White, hairy and manipulative. I walk away, living him enjoy his time in this world. On Monday morning, I see Leyla again.

"I missed you, Keevan. Let's hangout this Friday night. At my place if you don't mind." I look at her face, studying her dark brown eyes. "I would love to, but I'm not sure if I am going to be free by then." I reply, feeling guilty. I am not occupied by that time. I just want to be alone, surrounded with peace and noiselessness. She looks at mc sadly as if she is going to magically convince me into doing what she asked me to do. I am man of my words. Unconvinced. "How about we go to the local coffeeshop next Sunday morning?" she asks. Poor Leyla, oblivious to my introversion. "I will try" I reply, knowing that I won't even try.

She continues cleaning the supermarket all day long. We don't have many customers. Just a bunch of locals, visiting to buy their needs, formed by several economic and political systems. I sometimes listen to music on my phone when the store is empty. I listen to Rock music a lot despite the fact that it makes me depressed. Sometimes, depression feels similar to joy. One month later, Leyla starts flirting with me. I know she likes me, but the problem is that I can't like her, in a romantic way. Leyla and I go to the same local college and we both study English literature. We both are 20 years old and we work at the same place. Definitely not a coincidence. Maybe the universe is showing me signs. One night at 7 pm, an hour before my bedtime, I decide to go for a walk around the neighborhood. I pass by all the neighboring houses, each window showing anonymous silhouettes of people with different stories. A couple fighting in the kitchen, a what looks like a teenage girl playing with her pet dog, an old lady praying in her living-room. Unsimilar stories, same goals. All what they are aiming for is happiness. A state formed by chemicals and hormones. I listen to music as I am walking, trying to kill the presence of loneliness.

I moved out when I was 18. My parents weren't thrilled with the idea since we don't live in the west. "No one will cook for you, my son." my mom would say. "I know you want to move out so you can do whatever you like, especially the religiously forbidden stuff." my dad told me, aggressively. "My son, please reconsider your choices" my mom used to say to me. "you are our only child, Keevan".

Frankly speaking, I sometimes regret moving out, disconnecting myself from my very kind parents. It never was a good decision nor a socially constructed path for me. Nonetheless, I would not consider it a mistake. It was a choice, a product of my liberation.

One month later, Leyla confessed to me in the supermarket. "I love you" she said, wholeheartedly.

"I don't know what to say, but I really appreciate it, Leyla." I think that was a cold statement now that I think about it. It came out of my mouth consciously but it was undeliberate. I am awkward, a state of unstableness constantly hovering upon me. Leyla started loving me two years ago. She would flirt with me in a respective manner but alas, it was not attractive. It was vague. I have not always understood love as a concept. I have an unclear perspective on it. Based on what I have seen in romantic movies, it seems boring. Unsatisfying. Pointless. Maybe I am wrong because I have never been in love. Not that I can remember now. I only love God and my parents. That's the definition of love which I can comprehend.

Two weeks later, Leyla and I went for a walk in the local park early in the morning when the air was fresh and the weather was extremely cold. "Do you understand how I feel for you?" she asked, knowing that I am not ready for those types of questions. "No." I whispered, facing her. I told her the truth. "You are not taught what love is, my dear Keevan." she said. I was not hurt. I was just unfamiliar with the concept of romantic love, the one that occurs between couples. Maybe it's a part of my cognitive fragility.

One Saturday afternoon, as I was drinking my tea, my doorbell rang. I opened the door to see a delivery guy with a box in his hands.

I brought the box inside and opened it with curiosity.

There were two small books inside. They both were romantic novels. Leyla.

There are days which the air is filled with a heavy sadness. I feel very confused and I don't know what to do. Everything feels unfamiliar. Leyla's love for me, my parents love for me, my work, my boss, my life. Death. The only form of existence within my flat is me. I don't even have plants. Real ones I mean. No wonder why the air feels heavy in my room.

One month later, we go for a walk again. Leyla and I. the unparted couple. We are not a romantic couple. I don't have feelings for her. I barely have feelings except depression. Is it a feeling though?

I have been working for two years now, same position, same place, same boss and same atmosphere. A change would be a luxury for me, an alternation of my life. Yesterday evening, Leyla came up to me and whispered something uncomprehensive, scary and threatening. "You need to love me back." she said. Why is she so obsessed with me?

Leyla Abraham is from a small town which is nearly 45 kilometers far from the town which we currently live in. our town is green, full of flowers. When you walk in the streets you can easily smell lavender. The residents are annoyingly hygienic as if being extremely clean will cease their aging process and make them immortal. They are adorably kind, talkative and positive. My flat is next to a small mosque with a blue dome. On a weekend in December, Leyla surprisingly pays me a visit in the middle of the night. I open the door to see her sobbing, her mascara all over her cheeks, her eyes bloody red. She has been fired from her job. I give her a hug, not knowing how to comfort her. I let her sit on the burgundy sofa beside my bed. I bring her a cup of cinnamon tea. "I got fired from my job." she announces. I feel a wave of misery entering the room, enslaving both Leyla and I. Melancholy.

"Do you know why that happened?" I ask.

"I have no idea." she cries.

"Bad things happen to good people." I say, regretting it the moment it comes out of my mouth.

"Do you think I will ever find a job again, Keevan?" she asks, acknowledging my facial expression.

"Affirmative." I reply.

"Can I stay at your place tonight?" she asks. Knowing the answer.

"Yes Leyla. Of course."

"Thank you, my love." she says.

A silence is born for 5 minutes.

Two weeks later, I found Leyla a job at a local flower shop, a position fitting her like a summer dress. Delicate and easy.

One day, I decide to visit her at the flower shop, a predicted visit.

"Why hello there, pretty girl." I shout.

"Oh, bless you. May your day be filled with happiness and joy." She replies, shyly. She is extremely sweet. I approach her as she is arranging the tulips. I feel like I love her at this moment. A temporary form of time. I give her a warm hug, making her smile widely.

"I missed you so much." She says to me

"I missed you too, gorgeous girl." I reply, feeling like a hypocrite. I don't have romantic feelings towards her. She has cut her hair a bit. She is a brunette. She is wearing a pair of mom jeans, a pair of old black sneakers, and a white blouse. She tries to stay as modest as possible. "I feel better when I dress like this." she said once. Rebellious. I was wearing the same black t-shirt and black jeans when I visited her. The way I dress isn't very important in my opinion. Garments are to cover us, not to decorate us or objectify us. In the end, we will all die one day, the clothes not being of a drop of importance. I am a temporary guy, designed to go the way of all flesh. The unknown waiting for us.

"How are you feeling?" I ask Leyla. Curious.

"Thank God, I feel much better, now that I have a job." She replies, appreciatively.

"Praise be." I speak.

She really is appreciative.

On a Saturday night, one month later, she invites me to her house for dinner, with her family obviously. Her mom, Diana, has cooked so much food. Her dad, Selim, is a tall and smart man. He appears to be very confident. Leyla's younger sister, Aida, has curls. She is 17 years old. "Please, have a seat." Says Diana, Leyla's mom. We sit in the living room for a while to talk some random bullshit about the town that we reside in. the awkwardness filling the air as the time passes. "Let's go to the table and start eating." Selim mandates. After the dinner, Leyla takes me up to her bedroom while her dad does the dishes and her mom reads her novel. In Leyla's bedroom, several types of decorations can be observed including a peace lily plant, a small Persian mat on the floor, and a bookshelf full of books with colored spines. she closes the door of her bedroom and her lips meet mine, a very unfamiliar feeling of joy and sadness is born withing my body. The hormones. She really does love me; she would sacrifice anything for me to reflect her feelings. A mirror of romance. I don't think that I will ever be able to do so.

"You are undoubtfully my everything." She tells me.

"Are you objectifying me?" I laugh.

"I am not, Keevan."

"I don't think it is of importance" I reply.

"You shall reflect my emotions"

"I am unable to do so" I tell her.

"Why not?" she asks, misery hovering upon her.

"Because I don't have feelings for you, romantic ones I mean.

A silence is formed in the room.

After the passing of a few seconds, she starts using her mouth again to create the cliché phrase of "I love you".

"My apologies, Leyla. I cannot love you back in that way."

At that moment, her mom enters the room without even knocking on the door. She brings us two cups of tea and some cookies. I like her, a lady to be respected. After she leaves the room, we start drinking the tea and we eat the cookies.

A few months later, one Sunday morning, I wake up to the sound of my door bell ringing, very early in the morning. I open the door to see Leyla wearing a long black dress. It demonstrates grieve in our culture.

"What are you doing here?" I ask her.

"My mom has passed away." she whispers, her green eyes filled with waves of tears, begging to be liberated.

"You are not telling me the truth, are you?"

"Keevan, I am telling the truth." Her voice breaking. She looks extremely pale and lifeless. It takes me a second to notice the black headscarf covering her head. She is telling the truth, emphasizing on the accuracy of the unhappy news she just announced. I give her a hug. What a type of hug. An undeniable grieve washing over Leyla's entire existence. She looks small and fragile before my eyes. She tells me later that her mom had breast cancer. She was 45 years old. Lovely Diana. I cannot believe the sorrowful news I heard from Leyla. May she rest in peace. Death is inevitable, an instance of no physical form which cannot be manipulated.

In the following week, I go to the local mosque to Diana's funeral. A couple of days later, I visit Leyla and her family. They all seem breakable like the windows of an abandoned church, an object waiting for its destiny to be perished.

"I am so sorry for your loss." I announce.

"Thank you, Keevan." Her sister and her dad reply, simultaneously.

Leyla doesn't reply. Instead, she stares at the open window of the living room, blocked by light curtains. After a couple minutes of silence, she forms a word.

"Momentary." She speaks.

I think I understand her.

She stands up and walks over to the bathroom, closing the door with a thud. She stays silent inside. Nothingness.

The grieve is real, undeniable.

A couple of weeks later, I visit the flower shop, only to discover that she has left her job.

"She left the job after her mom passed away." A guy says.

"Oh, unsatisfactory news." I say with a low voice.

"Indeed." He affirms.

After I exit the store, I call her on the public phone. She doesn't pick it up. I call her again, twice and thrice. Still no response. I stare at my own reflection on the store's glass for two minutes straight. The guy who works there comes out and asks if I am alright. "I am very fine, thank you." I tell him. He seems a bit concerned, his face shaped into an incomprehensible structure of anxiety. It looks dreadful. In the afternoon of the same day, I decide to go back to my own flat. I take a shower and a nap too.

When I wake up, I see my room's window open, a bird sitting on my desk. It looks happy as if someone has accidentally spilled a can of serotonin on the bird's head. I wish I could relate.

At 6 pm, I receive a phone call from Leyla.

"I'm sorry." she says.

"Sorry for what?"

"For my attitude." She says to me, sounding as if she is falling down a deep hole.

"You have not done anything wrong." I reply.

"I might have done so."

"Not that I have observed." I reply.

She hangs up. I feel a very strange wave of emotions, misery and confusion. It feels like I have done something terrible even though I have no idea at all regarding what I have committed. Ignorance is a bliss.

Two months later, I got fired from my job. I felt terrible that day, a gap in my life becoming empty for emotional distress. Maybe my attachment to my job was built up with difficulty. It was hard to break it into smaller pieces.

One Friday evening, my 70 years old neighbor knocks on my door. When I open it, I see her standing with her veiny hands, holding a plate of Baklavas and some other sweets. Her name is Farida. She is 70 years old.

"Good evening my dear Keevan." She says.

"Good evening my dear, welcome, please come in and have a sit" I reply.

"Thank you so much, but I have to go back. My grandchildren are waiting for me." She says and hands me the plate. A benevolent lady she is.

"Please have a great evening." I reply back.

I have been living in this block for two years now, surrounded by the nicest people to ever exist. It's a domestic heaven. It's an unperceived privilege to be here. Everyone looks really happy here. I wish I could be as happy as they are. A state of feeling I am aiming to

reach. A greater worldly goal of all creatures.

2 months later, I heard the heart-breaking news of my neighbor's death, Farida's death. It feels like the angel of death is becoming an unwelcomed friend of mine, taking the intangible form of existence of my very beloved acquaintances without my consent, not that I would let him do so.

I started working in a local bookstore, breathing the smell of books every day, each smell telling a different story. The people who often visit the bookstore are the local residents, some from my own block, coming here to purchase a book they like to read, be it a religious one or a fictional one. It does not matter. Since I have started working at the bookstore, I have noticed how some people come to check the books, sit and read a few pages, some people finish a whole book in one sit in the bookstore. They are attached to what they read, believing every vague detail they read about, lost in them, their thoughts are flexible, adjustable and vulnerable to any changes of ideologies and beliefs. They seem very susceptible to me. They simple are attached. The wrong type of attachment. Is there a right way of attachment?

A couple of days later, Leyla and I decide to go for a walk in the local park. We go there because its peaceful. No human interactions, no noises, its only us, a pair of humans with different histories and tales. A tale of two humans.

"I have stopped having feelings towards you, Keevan." She announces with a monotone voice.

"What are you trying to convey?"

she looks at me, studying my face and all the blemishes I have on my façade. She looks manipulative.

"We are moving to the UK." She speaks.

For a moment, I am left with no words, my thoughts drifting away from me as far as possible, I feel something hurting in my throat. What am I feeling? I don't even have feelings towards her. A voice of despair and hopelessness echoes in my mind. It was the attachment that constructed this path for me. The wrong type of attachment, leading me the wrong way. I have developed the incorrect feelings, powerless to get rid of them. I have been blind, I don't know where my future is, lost in the desert of emotions, abandoned by the universe. But is it heaven up there?

"Good luck" I muttered. The time has come. It was all a temporary issue. Momentary.

This book doesn't have the acknowledgement part.

This is Shwan Fraidoon Abdulqader's first book.

Shwan goes by the name (Schwan Fereidun) on social media platforms.

www.ingramcontent.com/pod-product-compliance
Lightning Source LLC
Chambersburg PA
CBHW071234140726
47996CB00007B/2603